D1509065

MIKE FINK

by
Carol Beach York

illustrated by
Ed Parker

Folk Tales of America

Troll Associates

PROLOGUE

In the early years of our country—before the railroads were built, before the truckers were rolling—most supplies and goods were carried by riverboats.

Legends grew about the adventures of the riverboat men. And through the years, the stories attached themselves to one particular name: Mike Fink.

There may or may not have been a riverboat man by that name. But Mike Fink became a symbol for all the people who ever poled keelboats on the Ohio and Mississippi Rivers—rough, tough people who weren't afraid of anything. People who lived hard and worked hard on the rivers of our country when it was new.

Library of Congress # 79-66315
ISBN 0-89375-302-5/0-89375-301-7 (pb)

Mike Fink was born just about the same time the country was. And, soon after, he was ready for anything that happened. A new, growing country needs strong, bold people, so it was a good thing Mike came along when he did.

Take, for instance, the *Mississippi River Trouble.*

The trouble with the Mississippi was that there was just too much bad weather. An ornery old alligator was stirring up the waters with a tail as long as a mountain is high. It could whip up a mighty fierce storm. Even the sturdiest pioneer hesitated to cross the river. Families in covered wagons came to a halt on the east bank of the Mississippi and would go no farther. The settling of the West came to a standstill. Things were in a fine mess—until Mike Fink took charge.

Mike wasn't afraid of *anything,* not even that ornery alligator. He jumped right into the stormy waters one day, tied up the alligator's tail with a heavy rope, and walked back to shore, dripping wet and boasting for all to hear.

"I'm the snapping turtle of the O-hi-o. My boat's the *Lightfoot,* and I can lick any man or any alligator on any river any time!"

After that, the weather calmed down on the Mississippi, and the pioneers were willing to cross. Thanks to Mike Fink, the West got settled after all. You can go out there and see for yourself.

Besides being an alligator tamer, Mike Fink was a fearless scout and a crack shot with a rifle. His aim was so good that he could flick mosquitoes off fence posts and drive nails into barn doors. Mike called his rifle "Bang-All." Everybody knew that Mike Fink and Bang-All couldn't be beat.

Mike grew up in Pennsylvania country. He'd never had much time for schooling, so people sometimes thought he talked funny. But he was the best shot anywheres about. He had the strongest muscles, the bushiest mustache, and the fanciest squirrel-tail cap. He could jump higher, swim faster, yell louder, and spit farther than anyone around. If you didn't believe it, you could just ask Mike.

At the time of the Mississippi Trouble, Mike was a riverboat man. This is how it happened.

The brand new United States of America was beginning to grow and stretch out all over. And rivers were the roads of the country. If farm people wanted flour for biscuits or cloth for a shirt or dress, it came to them on the riverboats. Wheat, corn, cider, and salt, planks, hogs, gunpowder, kegs of nails, and barrels of molasses were carried along the river from

town to town on the riverboats—keelboats, flatboats, barges.

One day Mike got to talking with some riverboat men. They were loading cargo for a trip down the Ohio to New Orleans. Their muscles bulged as they worked. Knives glittered on their leather belts. They were strong, tough workers, and they didn't take second place to anybody, not even a fearless scout and crack rifle shot.

"Maybe scoutin' is risky work," one of the riverboat men said to Mike, "but the river's harder."

"Harder!" Mike tightened his muscles.

The riverboat man was sunburned and weatherbeaten and very tall. He looked at Mike a moment and then tossed a bundle of fur pelts into the cargo cabin as easy as a bundle of feathers.

"I can hold off sixty men at once," Mike shouted. "I can wrassle ten bears at a time. I'm half wildcat and half solid rock, and the rest of me's as hard as an iron skillet."

The boatmen went on loading their cargo as if they hadn't even heard all this wonderful news.

"We got lots to fight along the river, too," the captain said. "We got storms and whirlpools and floodwaters. And gettin' back upriver is hard work every bit of the way."

"Not too hard for me!" Mike roared. "I'm ready for anything!"

"Get aboard then," the riverboat captain said. He was laughing to himself. But he didn't laugh long. Mike Fink was born to be a riverboat man.

When Mike joined up with the keelboat crew, he soon found out what hard work meant. Going downstream along the Ohio to the Mississippi was bad enough. There were sandbars and floating trees, uprooted by storms and blown into the river. The sandbars could hang up a boat, and the ragged ends of tree roots could tear a hole right through the hull.

But downstream, at least the boat was going with the flow of the river. It was after the men delivered their goods in New Orleans and started back up the Mississippi that Mike really saw some hard work.

Now the river was against them. The men rowed when the water was deep, and when it was shallow they poled the boat along. They stood on the boat deck and drove the ends of their long poles into the river bed, and *pushed*.

Each push sent the boat ahead a little. But it was a slow, hard haul every bit of the way. Tough men were needed, and Mike Fink was the toughest.

Mike took to riverboat life so fast that it wasn't long before he had his own boat. He built it all in one day and named it the *Lightfoot*. Then he hired his own crew.

Mike Fink needed only a crew of six instead of sixteen, because he was as strong as ten people all by himself. He rowed hard and he poled hard. And when he went ashore, he danced hard and fought hard and generally stirred things up a mite. Everybody knew when Mike Fink was in town.

"I'm a salt-river roarer!" Mike would yell when he hit town. "I'm half wild horse and half cockeyed alligator! And I'm ready for anything!"

Sometimes Mike stirred things up a mite too much, like the time of the Hundred Men Fight. People are still talking about *that*.

The strongest, wildest, rowdiest fighters came from miles around to challenge Mike Fink. Trappers came out of the woods. Scouts and hunters came, too—along with husky farmers and powerful riverboat men.

"Mike, I heard Hard-Head Pierce is comin'
all the way from Pittsburgh to show you who's
the best fighter," a flatboat captain told Mike.

"I'm ready for anything!" Mike yelled.
"Come on, Hard-Head!"

Hard-Head came on all right. All the way
from Pittsburgh. His way of fighting was to
lower his head and rush at the other man like
an angry billy goat.

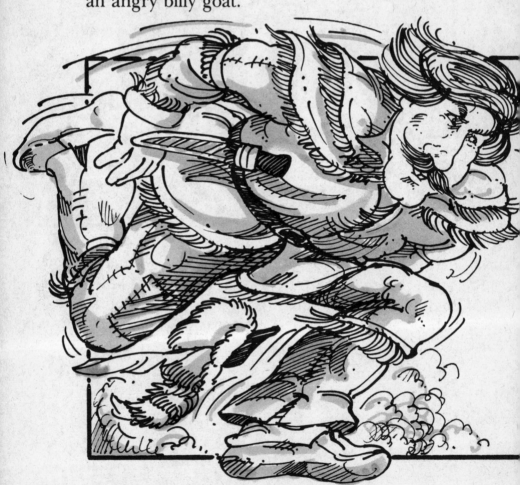

Mike took one look at Hard-Head coming at him head first, and then he lowered his own head and charged straight on.

A crowd had gathered in the field to watch the fighting, and a great cheer went up. When the two heads met, Mike Fink sent Hard-Head flying. Hard-Head Pierce landed smack up in a tree. When he came wobbling down, he had a lump on his head the size of a pumpkin. And a new name—Tree-Top Pierce.

Next in line was Iron-Fist Harry.

"Mike can't beat him," the crowd agreed. "Iron-Fist will flatten Mike in one blow!"

Mike tightened his jaw, and Iron-Fist Harry struck.

What got flattened was Harry's hand, and after that he was known as—that's right, Flat-Fist Harry.

Then came the Whipper brothers, Quick-Legs and Long-Legs. The crowd cheered and booed and stamped.

"Come on!" Mike roared. "I ain't tired yet!"

Quick-Legs moved around so fast that nobody ever caught up with him. He'd never been beat because he'd never been hit.

But Mike Fink was quicker. His punches went out so fast and steady that everywhere Quick-Legs moved, a punch was already there waiting for him. Quick-Legs collapsed in a heap.

Now the crowd rushed on to another section of the field to see Mike fight the other Whipper brother. Long-Legs was so tall that nobody could reach up high enough to land a punch on his jaw. He'd never been beat because he'd never been hit.

"You're licked for sure now, Mike," the onlookers shouted.

"First, I'll lick Long-Legs," Mike bellowed, "and then I'll lick everyone who says I'm licked."

Mike tossed his squirrel-tail cap in the air and jumped up to catch it. He had time to give Long-Legs twenty-two blows before he touched ground again.

So it went all day long. Mike Fink fought a hundred men, and Mike Fink won a hundred times. He had to quit at last because there was nobody left standing up to fight him anymore.

Mike was feeling pretty good by then. He went swaggering through town with the crowd following him, cheering and yelling and making more commotion than ever.

So Mike's fame spread far and wide—up and down the rivers, through the wild country, into the smallest towns, and out to the trading posts. They said he won all the riverboat races, and he tied up the alligator's tail. He could beat anyone at anything.

And since all that was true, it might come as a surprise to learn that once, just once, Mike Fink lost a contest. Folks couldn't believe it. But it's a fact. And they still talk about it to this day.

It all began with the Big Contest Week planned at Fast Water, Ohio. Now, considering how good Mike was at *everything*, it's no wonder that nobody wanted him to know about Big Contest Week.

Fast Water wasn't much of a town. It was hardly a town at all—just one street, a few cabins, and a general store. Folks thought things might perk up a bit if they could attract some attention to Fast Water. Big Joe Bucker thought up Big Contest Week, and he put himself in charge. There would be contests of every kind. If Mike Fink came, he would surely win them all without any trouble. So everybody said they'd keep it a secret.

Well, it's hard to keep anything as big as Big Contest Week a secret—and, sure enough, word leaked out. It was Skinny Owens who spilled the beans, and Big Joe Bucker never forgave him.

Skinny ran into Mike and his crew early one morning. The men had tied up the *Lightfoot* and were sleeping on shore, just as they did every night. When Skinny Owens came along, Mike was the only one awake. Since they were a long way from Fast Water, Skinny couldn't resist mentioning the big event. He thought it was a good joke on Mike.

"Too bad you won't be in Fast Water tomorrow for Big Contest Week," Skinny said, smart-like.

"What Big Contest Week?" Mike always cocked an ear whenever he heard the word "contest."

"Joe Bucker's Big Contest Week," Skinny said. "Fightin', shootin', everything."

"Who says I won't be there?" Mike was already on his feet.

Skinny weighed about four hundred pounds, and every pound was quivering with pure pleasure to see Mike getting so riled up. "It'll take more'n a week of hard polin' to get to Fast Water," Skinny said. "By that time, the contest will be over."

But Mike wasn't wasting any more time listening to Skinny Owens.

27

"Man the oars, boys!" he shouted to his crew.

The crew wasn't very wide awake, but they jumped around as fast as they could. They forgot about breakfast, untied the *Lightfoot,* and began to row and pole their way upstream toward Fast Water, with Mike at the steering oar.

Now Mike only had one day to get to Fast Water. It was a week's trip, even with the best conditions, and he didn't run into any "best conditions." Sandbars and fallen trees seemed to be everywhere in the river that spring. But Mike dug in his pole and pushed so hard that the *Lightfoot* skimmed over the water and over every bit of trouble in its way.

It was a marvelous sight to behold. People gathered on the river banks to watch the *Lightfoot* whizz by, zipping over the sandbars and broken trees like a grasshopper.

"We'll make it, boys," Mike sang out. "The *Lightfoot* ain't even touchin' water this trip!"

And that was just about the truth of it.

The boat was halfway to Fast Water when a terrible storm came up. It looked like Mike was going to have to quit. Waves rose so high that

the men were looking down at the tops of the trees along the shore. Thunder cracked so loud that it sounded like Judgment Day had come early. Lightning flashed and lit up the river like fireworks.

"I ain't givin' up!" Mike roared. And he went right on until he came to Fast Water, riding so high on the storm waves that the *Lightfoot* almost washed right up onto the main street of town.

Mike shook the water from his squirrel-tail cap and stepped off his boat in front of the general store.

"Here I am!" he hollered. "I'm here to win, and I'm ready for anything!"

It was the first day of the contests, and a group had already gathered in a clearing nearby. They were waiting for the storm to let up so they could shoot up their own storm. But when they saw Mike Fink and Bang-All, they put down their rifles. Even Sarah Bucker, Big Joe's cousin, gave up. She was Fast Water's best shot. But there was no sense even *trying* to outshoot Mike.

Big Joe Bucker tried to rally everybody.

"We've got to make the best of things," he declared. "Mike Fink can't win *every* contest."

You've heard of "famous last words"? Well, you just heard some more of them right there.

After the shooting match was called off, the group broke up. Half the people said they were going on home, now that Mike Fink had come.

The next day was the fighting contest. And it wasn't much. Hard-Head Pierce still had the bump on his head and couldn't fight. Flat-Fist Harry hung back behind a tree. The Whipper brothers never showed up at all.

It went the same all week long.

There was a jumping contest. But Mike
could jump clear across the Ohio River and
back again, so nobody challenged him. The
swimming contest and the fishing contest came
to nothing. Mike swam the Ohio with his an-
kles tied together, and he just "talked" the fish
right up out of the river. When the day of the
dancing contest came, none of the men even
bothered to get out of bed. Mike danced all
day without stopping once. His dancing
partners were tuckered out afterward, but
Mike felt just fine.

He twirled the curly ends of his black mustache and said, "I'm just warmin' up. What's the contest tomorrow?"

"Eating," one of the young women said politely. She thought Mike was very handsome.

But Mike didn't notice. He was thinking about food.

"Eatin' contest! That's mighty good news. Dancin' works up an appetite. I can eat a barn full of food."

You might think that would have scared away the others, Mike saying he could eat a barn full of food. But riverboat crews have appetites like bears in a honey log, and they all thought they could eat at least as much as Mike Fink. This was one contest all the men thought they could win. So, they came out for the eating contest, and on came the food.

The first course was roast turkey. Mike ate three. He could have eaten more, but the next course was biscuits and gravy, and that was a special favorite of his. After the biscuits and gravy, there was rabbit stew and hot potatoes. There were buckets of corn, platters of fish, and pails of berries.

The other men began to groan and loosen their belts. By and by, they couldn't eat one more crumb. Only Big Joe Bucker and Mike were left. Big Joe stood near high as a big tree, and he had a lot of space to fill. He sat grinning at Mike across the plank table and shoveling in the food.

"Bring it on!" he called.

"Bring me *twice* as much!" Mike roared back.

Deer meat, bear meat, cornbread, squash, hotcakes, pea soup, bacon, beans . . . and then more roast turkey.

Big Joe Bucker began to get red in the face.

He loosened his belt.

He stopped shouting for more.

He rested on the table.

And he finally quit eating.

Mike washed everything down with five gallons of cider, and won another contest.

That night some of the townspeople gathered at Big Joe Bucker's cabin. They were glum and gloomy, fit to be tied, and ready to kill Skinny Owens.

Mrs. Big Joe Bucker sat knitting quietly in a corner. Nobody paid much mind to her until she spoke up after a bit.

"It appears to me that this Mr. Fink is very active."

"Active! Well, that's a fact." Everybody had to smile at that, even as discouraged as they felt.

"It appears to me that it would be very hard for Mr. Fink to sit still for very long," she said.

"Couldn't do it," they agreed.

Mrs. Bucker didn't say another word. She just sat rocking and knitting and smiling to herself. Everybody looked around at one another. One by one, they began to grin. Then they began to laugh. Big Joe caught up his wife and gave her a walloping kiss.

"You're the smartest woman this side of the Ohio or any other river!" he cried.

The next morning a notice was posted at the general store.

SITTING-STILL CONTEST
COMMENCES AT NOON
EVERYBODY WELCOME

Now some of the men and women were afraid that Mike wouldn't enter. But, as Big Joe Bucker told them, "Mike Fink can't resist entering any kind of contest, *ever.*"

And Big Joe was right. Mike read the sign that morning. He didn't look like he liked the idea much. But Mike Fink just couldn't turn down any contest, *ever.*

And so it began.

Everything was real quiet and still. Those in

the contest were all sitting like mice, and the rest were off to the side, just watching. Two minutes passed. Three minutes passed. Then five. Everybody was sitting very still.

The watchers began to look at each other. Could Mrs. Big Joe Bucker have been wrong about Mike Fink?

Two more minutes passed. Another minute passed. Some people sighed, and some people frowned. It looked like another bad day for Big Contest Week.

And then it happened! Exactly eight and one-half minutes after the contest started, Mike Fink couldn't stand it any longer. He jumped to his feet with a mighty shout.

"I'm a salt-river roarer!" he yelled. "I'm half wild horse and half cockeyed alligator! I'm a ready-for-anything man. But I just can't sit still!!"

Sleepy McGee won the contest (two hours and three minutes). But some folks say he was asleep half the time, so it didn't count.

After that, Big Contest Week came to an end.

The last contest was poling away from town, and all the riverboat men lined up along the bank with their boats.

Mike aimed to finish his glorious week in style after the sitting-still setback. He shoved his pole so hard that the *Lightfoot* shot all the way down the Ohio and into the Mississippi. Some say clear to New Orleans.

Folks could hear him shouting as he went down the river. "I'm ready for anything," he yelled. "I'm ready to outjump, outfight, outrow, outpole, outdance, outsmart, outshoot, and outeat anyone alive!"

Yes, Mike Fink was a ready-for-anything man. Except, of course, for sitting still.